Look up into the sky. Can you see the rainbow? It arches like a bridge over the hills and comes down into Nutshell Wood. At the end of the rainbow, deep in the wood, a tiny magical village is appearing. That village is Rainbow's End. Rainbow's End can only be seen by humans when a rainbow is in the sky, otherwise it is invisible to everyone except the gnomes who live there and the woodland animals.

The gnomes of Rainbow's End are jolly little folk who are always busy. Lots of exciting and interesting things happen in the village and no one is ever bored. This book tells the story of something that happened there. A little bird told me!

Rainbow's End

TOBY CLAYPOT'S WISHING WELL

Written by Jane Patience
Illustrated by John Patience

PUBLISHED BY PETER HADDOCK LIMITED
BRIDLINGTON, ENGLAND

High up in a tree in Rainbow's End, lived a mischievous magpie. His nest was large and untidy and filled with things which he had stolen from the town over the hills. The gnomes of Rainbow's End would have been amazed to see these things – there were rings big enough for a gnome to wear as bracelets, a silver brooch with a jewel in it as big as a gnome's fist and a teaspoon as large as a soup ladle. These things belonged to humans, and humans were something the gnomes did not know existed.

At the foot of the magpie's tree there was an old clay flowerpot. This too had come from the human town, but had not been brought by the magpie. The stream had carried it to Rainbow's End many years ago and it had been found by a gnome called Toby. This was very good luck for Toby since the tree in which he had his home had recently been blown down in a terrible storm. As soon as he saw the flowerpot Toby knew that it would make a fine new home. After a few minor alterations, which were easy

for Toby because he was Rainbow's End's odd-job gnome, he was able to move in. From that day, he was always known as Toby Claypot. Now, many years later, Toby still did all the odd jobs although he was very old. In fact, it would soon be his one hundred and second birthday.

Like the other gnomes in the town, Toby Claypot had to get all his water from the spring. The water here was sweet and fresh, but oh! dear, what a mess the place was in. With the constant flow of water and the trampling feet of all the gnomes who came there each day, the ground was always terribly muddy. The boots and shoes of all the folk who used the spring got plastered with the awful sticky mud and everyone complained about it. One day, as he was waiting his turn at the spring, Toby Claypot had an idea. ''Perhaps I could make some sort of well,'' he said. ''With a proper wall around and a bucket to collect the water in.'' Everyone thought it was a marvellous idea.

After a few days of hard work, Toby had finished the new well. It really did look splendid. It had a low stone wall around it and its own little roof. There was even a bucket to collect the water in. All the folk were very pleased with their new well, because it meant an end to muddy boots and shoes!

Toby Claypot's 102nd birthday drew nearer and nearer. One day his little granddaughter came to see him in his flowerpot home. Her name was Primrose and she loved visiting her grandfather because his house was so interesting. For one thing, it was made out of a huge flowerpot, whereas most gnomes live in trees. And, it was always full of such interesting things. As Toby was odd-job gnome, all the other gnomes brought him things to repair and these were scattered all over his house. As they sat together in his workshop, Toby and Primrose were talking about the new well. "Everyone is very pleased with it, Grandad," the little girl said. "And so they should be," Toby replied. "After all, it is a wishing well, you know." And he winked.

The next day Primrose was playing at home in her own garden. She tried to play with her toys, but she couldn't stop thinking about her Grandad's birthday. "I would love to give him a present," she said to her dolls. "But how can I? I haven't anything to give. Oh I wish, I wish, I wish . . ." Then she had an idea. "Of course," she said excitedly, "Grandad said it was a wishing well, so perhaps if I make a wish there, it may come true."

Primrose hurried to the well. She decided that the best way to make a wish was to do it while drinking the wishing well water. (She was quite right about this.) Carefully, she drew up the heavy bucket and, scooping out a handful of the sparkling water, she sipped it, closed her eyes tightly and wished. "I wish, I wish for a present for Grandad." Just as Primrose was wishing, the magpie was flying back from the town over the hill. In his beak he was carrying a gold pocket watch. Suddenly the watch slipped and fell, spinning down, down, down through the air and fell with a splash into the bucket of water. Primrose bent forward and looked in. "An enormous gold watch," she exclaimed. "My wish has come true!"

At last, the day of Toby Claypot's birthday arrived and Primrose hurried round to see her Grandad. She had wrapped the watch very carefully and had been looking forward to giving it to him. "Happy birthday, Grandad," she said as he opened the door. And then she held out her special present. "My goodness me," he cried when he saw the splendid gold watch. "This will look lovely on the wall, above the fireplace. Thank you, Primrose, it's marvellous but where ever did you get it from?" "I wished for it at your wishing well," replied Primrose. Toby scratched his head and wondered – but he never found out where the watch really came from, only the magpie knew that!

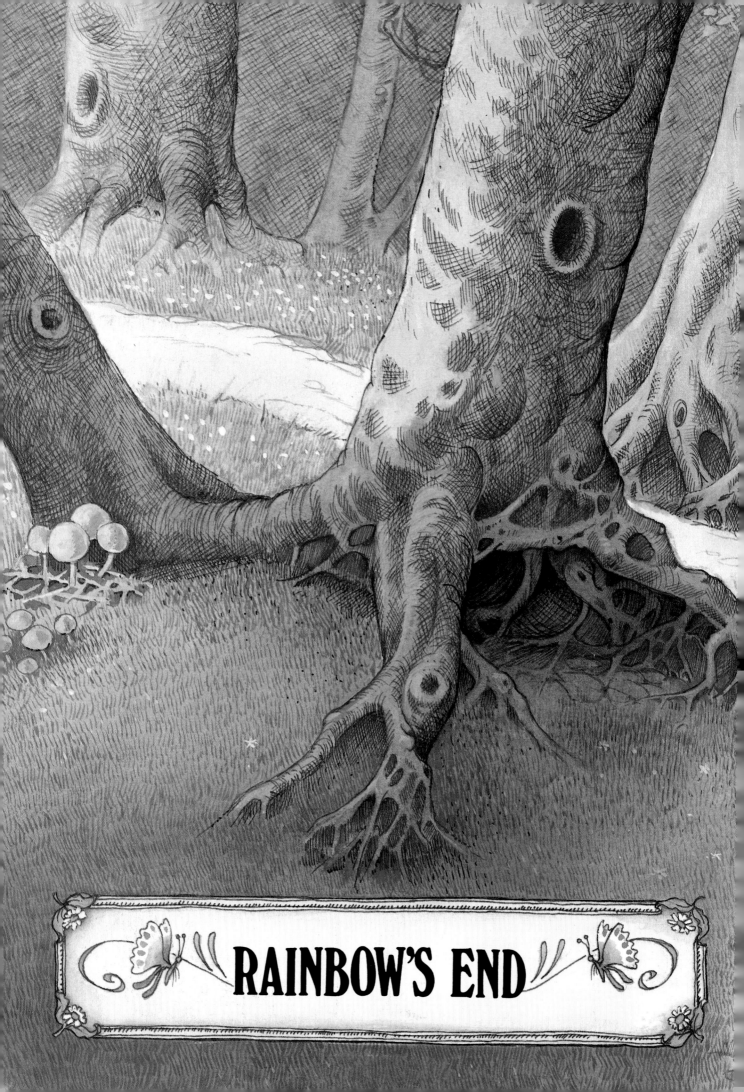

RAINBOW'S END